Printed in the United States of America

First Edition
1 3 5 7 9 10 8 6 4 2

Library of Congress Catalog Card Number on file

ISBN 0-7868-4679-8

For more Disney Press fun, visit www.disneybooks.com

My Name Is JoJo

By Tennant Redbank

DISNEY PRESS

New York

Hi!
My name is JoJo.
I am a clown.

I have a pet lion.
We live in
Circus Town.

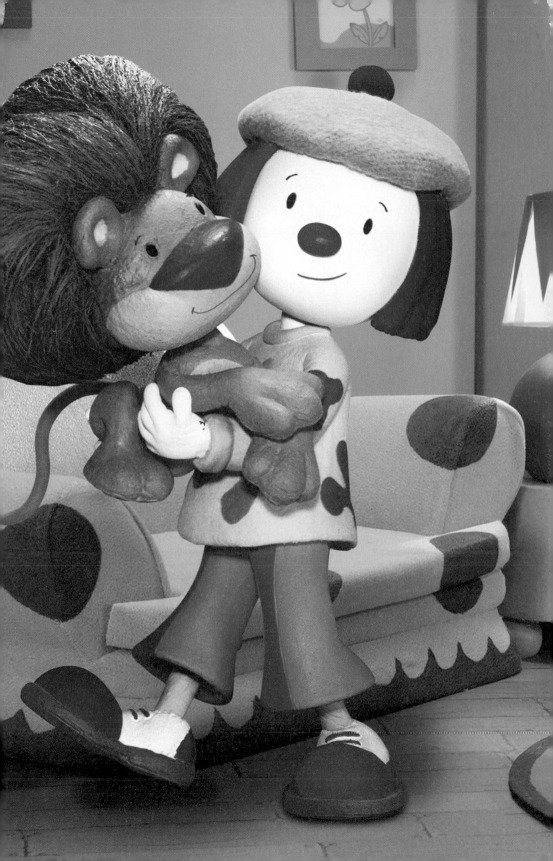

We jump

and run.

We dance

Meet my mom and dad.
They are in the show.
It is about to start.
It is time for us to go!

These green frogs
are fun to see.
Count them with me—
one, two, three!

Skeebo flips!

Trina twirls!

Dinky skips!

Bal Boa curls!

When I am grown up,
I will be a star.
And like my dad,
I will go far!

When I am done
I will take a bow.
See? I can do that
even now.